Roch

MR C

# Mr Croc's Walk

# Frank Rodgers

A & C Black • London

# Rockets

## MR CROC - Frank Rodgers

What Mr Croc Forgot
Mr Croc's Clock
Mr Croc's Walk
Mr Croc's Silly Sock

First paperback edition 1999
First published 1999 in hardback by
A & C Black (Publishers) Ltd
35 Bedford Row, London WC1R 4JH

Copyright © 1999 Frank Rodgers

The right of Frank Rodgers to be identified as author
and illustrator of this work has been asserted by
him in accordance with the Copyright, Designs
and Patents Act 1988.

ISBN 0-7136-5049-4

A CIP catalogue record for this book is available
from the British Library.

Printed and bound by G. Z. Printek, Bilbao, Spain.

It was Saturday morning and Mr Croc
was having his usual big breakfast.

3

As he ate, Mr Croc watched TV.
Miss Shape, the fitness lady, was on.
'It's a good idea to exercise in the
morning,' she said.

'I think I will,' said Mr Croc.
He picked up another
slice of toast and
wiggled his toes
as he ate.

Then he did
a knee-bend
as he slurped
his porridge.

After that he guzzled a plateful of fishfingers while touching his toes – 'Burp!' said Mr Croc.

'Walking is the best exercise,' said
Miss Shape.

Hiking and rambling fill you full of fresh air and energy!

'Yes!' said Mr Croc.

That's what I'll do! I'll go hiking!

He looked in the mirror and smiled his lovely smile.

Mr Croc thought he had the loveliest smile in the world.

Quickly he made himself a shopping list.
'First of all,' he said, 'I'll need a pair of
hiking boots.'

Then I'll need a tent and a map so I know where I'm going.

When he had
finished his
list, he put it
in his pocket
and set off
for the shops.

Outside the sports shop he met his
friend, Mr Hound.

'Hello, Mr Croc,' said Mr Hound.

Mr Croc had a terrible memory.

'Don't worry,' said Mr Hound. 'Perhaps
if we go into the shop you'll remember.'
So they went inside and Mr Croc
looked around.
'I want to do some exercise that will give
me lots of fresh air,' he said.

Mr Croc got on one of the bikes.
It started to move...

...and Mr Croc
started to
wobble.

He rolled towards a huge display of
footballs... but Mr Hound stopped him
just in time.

Mr Croc jumped off.
'I can't ride a bike,' he said.

Mr Croc put on
a helmet...

...and began to
climb the shop
ladder.

But near the top he began to wobble...

Ohhh...
I feel
dizzy!

Mr Hound helped him down.
'I'm afraid of heights,' said Mr Croc.

'Perhaps we should go outside for a
breath of air,' said Mr Hound.

'Yes... a walk,' replied Mr Hound.

'And I've just remembered something else,' said Mr Croc.

I made a list!

Mr Croc checked the list. Then he bought a tent...

...a pair of hiking boots...

...and a map. He also bought a stick to lean on and a woolly hat.

Mr Croc put on his hat and looked in the shop mirror. He smiled his lovely smile...

...and practised what to do when he met another hiker.

As he swept off his woolly hat, he
knocked into a
shop dummy,
sending
it flying.

Mr Hound sprang forward and caught it
just in time.

Mr Croc didn't even notice.

He was too busy smiling and waving his walking stick.

'Have a nice day,' he called, knocking a silver trophy from a shelf.

But once again, Mr Hound saved the day.

Mr Croc gathered up his parcels and hurried out of the shop. When they were safely outside Mr Hound sighed with relief.

When he got home Mr Croc packed his rucksack with food...

...sixteen sardine sandwiches...

...and twenty tins of tuna.

YUM!

Mr Croc liked fish.

He put on his
new boots...

...tied the
tent to his
rucksack...

...and checked himself in the mirror.

Mr Croc set off, breathing deeply as
he went.

After a while he looked at his map.
'I think I'll walk through the park,'
he said.

As he went through the gates he caught sight of his reflection in the window of the park keeper's cottage.

Mr Croc put his map down so he could adjust his woolly hat.

Then he set off again... forgetting all about the map.

When he got to the duck pond he sat down and took out his sardine sandwiches.

Just then Mr Green, the park keeper, arrived. He looked very glum.

'The children are sad because there are no ducks in the pond,' said Mr Green.

Mr Green pointed to the thick woods
all around the pond.
'The ducks don't know the pond is here,
they can't see it from the air,' he said.

Mr Croc gave a little smile.
'Well, as there are no ducks to feed, I'll
have to share my lunch with you!'

Mr Croc and Mr Green ate all the
sardine sandwiches.

Feeling refreshed, Mr Croc set off
again... into the woods.

But because he had no map, Mr Croc
soon got lost.
'Which way?' he thought. 'East... or west?'
He stopped and looked around.

Mr Croc unrolled his tent.

'Oops!' he said, 'I've forgotten to bring the tent pegs!'

Mr Croc looked around and found some branches.

When he had finished he smiled. 'Not bad,' he said. Then his tummy rumbled.

But when Mr Croc took the tins out of his bag he let out an even bigger groan.
'Oh, no!' he cried.

I've forgotten to bring a tin-opener!

Mr Croc's tummy rumbled again.
'Oh dear,' he said.

I'll just have to go to bed and try to forget all about food!

Mr Croc didn't sleep well that night. Not only did his tummy rumble, but the leaves rustled spookily in the wind, the branches tapped on the tent like scary fingers...

...and an owl hooted like a wailing ghost.

As soon as the sun came up Mr Croc
looked out of his tent.
It was still very windy but he didn't care.

But just as he said that...

...a great gust of wind lifted the tent into the air.

Oh no!

Mr Croc leapt to his feet and gave chase... but he couldn't catch it.

Higher and higher
went the tent...
flapping in
the wind.

Mr Croc chased it all the way to a pond
where he bumped into Mr Green.

'What are you doing back here?' asked
Mr Green.

'Where's your tent?' asked Mr Green.
Mr Croc pointed into the sky.

Mr Green looked up and gasped.

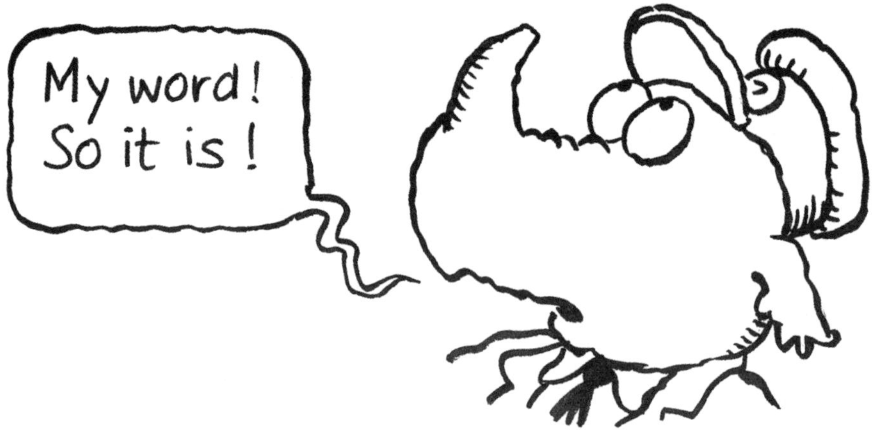
My word! So it is!

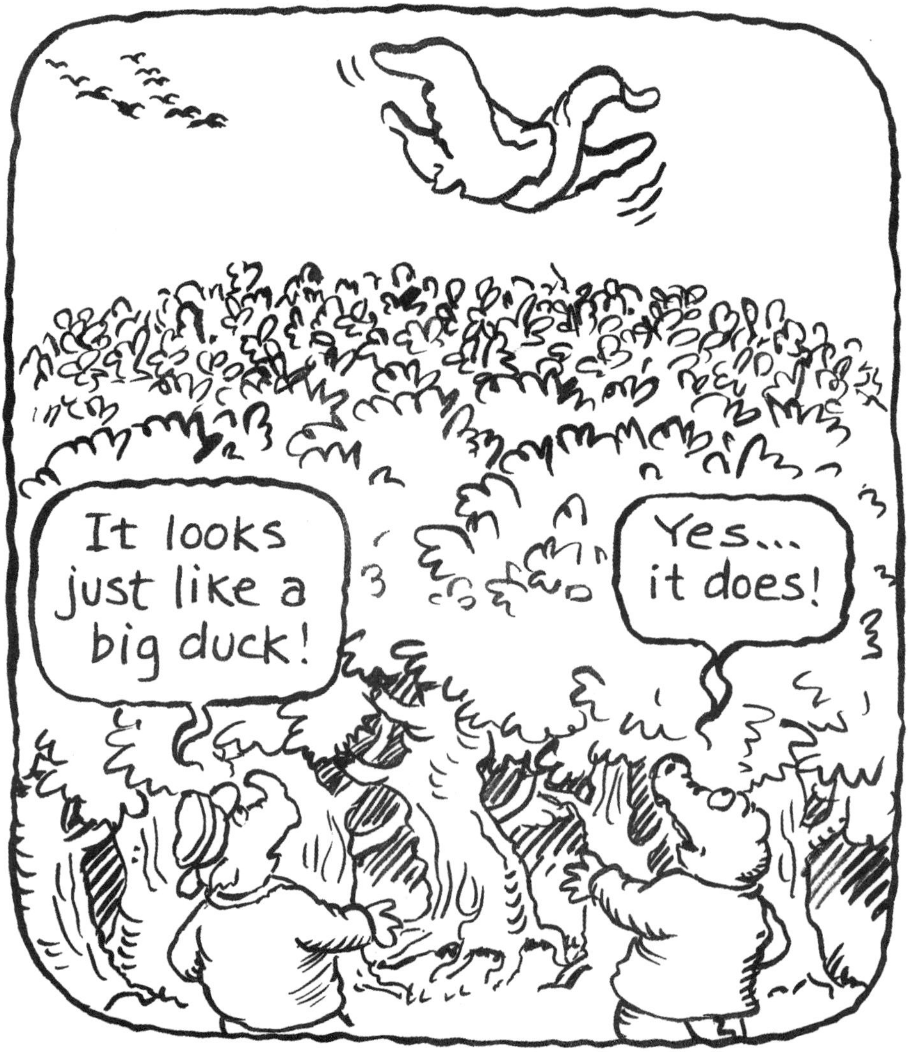
It looks just like a big duck!
Yes... it does!

Suddenly Mr Green pointed at the sky.

A flight of real ducks had appeared.

The leader must have thought that
Mr Croc's tent really was a *big* duck...

...because it turned and
flew towards it,
followed by the
other ducks.

At that moment the wind dropped and
the tent began to fall to the ground...
followed by the ducks.

Down, down flapped the tent until...

...it landed
in the
pond.

Then one after the other, all the ducks landed in the pond too.

Mr Green was overjoyed.

'It's wonderful, Mr Croc,' he cried.

'The duck pond is full of ducks again!'

'And it's all because of you, Mr Croc,'
he said. 'How can I ever repay you?'
Mr Croc's tummy rumbled loudly
and Mr Green smiled.

At the park keeper's cottage, Mr Green and his wife made Mr Croc the biggest breakfast he had ever had.

After breakfast Mr Croc fetched his rucksack. Then he and Mr Green helped the children to feed the ducks.

Mr Croc smiled his lovely smile and Mr Green shook his hand.

Mr Croc's lovely smile grew even wider.
'Back home,' he said.

## The End